Walking with Maga

All About Kids Publishing
6280 San Ignacio Ave., Suite C
San Jose, CA 95119
www.aakp.com

Editor: Lisa M. Tooker
Book Design: Kirsten Carlson

Printed in Hong Kong

For information about permission
to reproduce any selection from this book write to:

All About Kids Publishing
6280 San Ignacio Ave., Suite C
San Jose, CA 95119
www.aakp.com

Library of Congress Card Number: 00-111947
ISBN 0-9700863-4-2

Walking with Maga

written by Maureen Boyd Biro

illustrated by Joyce Wheeler

all about kids
publishing

san jose

For Martin, who always believed
—M.B.B.

For Craig
and "All the Girls"
—J.W.

When Maga and I go walking, we don't walk very fast.

There is too much to see.

A chipmunk, climbing a sycamore branch.
Birds perched high on a wire.
A yellow house.
Forget-me-nots.
A snail. A hose. One red rose.

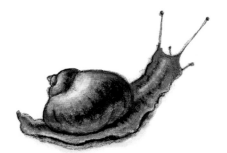

When Maga and I go walking,
we talk about things we like.

"Ice cream," I say, when it is hot.
"Cocoa," Maga says, when it is cold.
"Christmas," I sigh. I wish it were here.
"Peacocks!" Maga laughs.
"They look so grand."
"Like you," I answer, and take Maga's hand.

When Maga and I go walking,
we stop a lot to rest.

We sit on a bench and watch the clouds
float by in the April sky.
"I see a dragon," Maga says, pointing up.

"There's a wizard!"
"A monkey."
"A boot."

The sun on our skin is warm,
and lilacs in bloom scent the air.

When Maga and I go walking,
we visit people we know.

The lemon lady's two, full trees
are sweet and heavy with fruit.
She gives us a sack to carry home.
Later, we'll make lemonade.

We stop by Mr. Anton's garage.
It's filled with shells from the sea.
He picks up a starfish, prickly and orange.
He presses a shell to my ear.
"Listen," he says.
I do, and I hear the roar of the ocean inside.

"Come back tomorrow." He smiles and waves.
We will—and bring cookies we've baked.

When Maga and I go walking,
we joke as we poke along.
"What has two heads,
three hands, and four legs?" I ask,
then grin, and wait.

"Hmmm," Maga says.
She thinks. She frowns.
She shakes her head, and asks.
"What does have two heads,
three hands, and four legs?
A very odd creature, I'd say."

"It's us!" I cry.
"Just look." And we do,
at our shadows trailing behind.

"It's us, indeed,"
Maga says shuffling on.
Her shadow shuffles on too.

When Maga and I go walking,
we gather things we find.

A smooth, round stone.
A bottle cap.
Leaves, acorns, and bugs.

Maga lets a caterpillar crawl down her arm.
It's wrinkled and funny and slow.

"Like me," Maga laughs.
She scoops the bug up.
She places it in my hand.
It's warm and soft and full of life.

"Like you," I agree. I put it back gently,
and we walk a little further.

The autumn air is crisp and cool.
It rustles the leaves on the trees.

Maga spies a dandelion swaying in the grass.
"Let's make a wish," she says.

"I wish I could always go walking with you," I say.
Maga whispers, "Me too."

We close our eyes and bend our heads,
softly blowing the dandelion's seeds free.

The wind floats our wish up into the sky—

and Maga and I walk on.